BLUEY

GRANNIES

PENGUIN YOUNG READERS LICENSES
An imprint of Penguin Random House LLC, New York

First published in Australia by Puffin Books, 2020

First published in the United States of America by Penguin Young Readers Licenses, an imprint of Penguin Random House LLC, New York, 2021

This book is based on the TV series *Bluey*.

BLUEY™ and BLUEY character logos ™ & © Ludo Studio Pty Ltd 2018.
Licensed by BBC Studios. BBC logo ™ & © BBC 1996.

ISBN 9780593384169   09876543 2 COMM

Janet and Rita are heading to the shops.

3

The grannies cause chaos in Mum's corner store.
Rita forgets to pay for her beans again.

"Wake up, Janet!" says Mum.

JUST HAVING a nana nap, Love.

Rita makes a run for it, but slips on her beans.

Bingo jumps up, giggling, and begins to floss.

But Bluey doesn't think grannies can floss.

"Yeah, they can," replies Bingo.

They ask Mum
who is **RIGHT**.

Mum sighs.
"Ask your father."

They find Dad in the bathroom, unblocking the stinky toilet.

"How should I know if grannies floss?" he tells them.
"Go ask your nana."

Of course! Bluey and Bingo call Nana. If she can floss, then Bingo's **RIGHT**. But if she can't, Bluey's **RIGHT**.

Nana's ears answer.

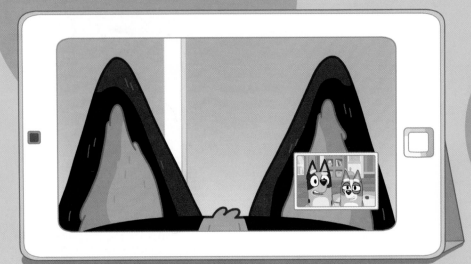

DOWN, Nana!

Then her feet.

UP, Nana!

10

Then her eyeball.

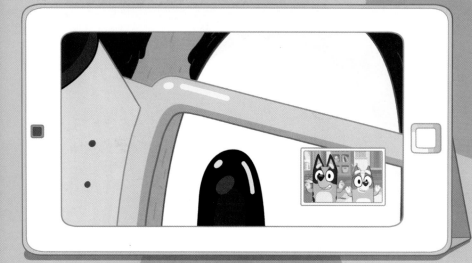

BaCK, Nana! BaCK!

HI, GIRLS!

Nana's not great with screens and things, but finally she works it out.

11

"...can you do the flossing dance?" asks Bingo.

"Well, I'll give it a go," says Nana.

She wibbles and wobbles, and flaps her arms around. Bobba joins her and starts to dance too, kicking his legs out to the sides.

It's dancing all right, but it's not flossing.

"I was **RIGHT!**" yells Bluey. "Grannies can't floss!"

Bluey wants to carry on playing, but Bingo doesn't feel like being a granny anymore. Bluey doesn't understand why and stomps off.

Mum suggests Bluey asks herself if she wants to be **RIGHT**, or if she wants the game to keep going. Because sometimes you can't have both.

But Bluey thinks you can.

I KNOW!

She makes another call.
"Nana, you're going to learn how to floss."

It's time to teach this old dog a new trick!

When Bluey is done, she surprises Bingo.

"Grannies **can** floss!" shouts Bingo.

"Yeah, I was wrong," says Bluey with a smile.

"Thanks, Bluey," says Bingo.
"Thanks, Nana."

YOU'RE WELCOME, BINGO.

"Let's play Grannies!" says Bluey.

LOVELY DAY FOR A DRIVE,
WOULDN'T YOU SAY, RITA?

SURE IS, JANET.

THUMP!

Rita and Janet might not be the best drivers,
but they sure know how to floss.
And that's way more fun than being **RIGHT**.